TEENAGE MUTANT NINJA TURTLES

Kevin Eastman and Peter Laird

Steve Lavigne
Letterer

Kevin Eastman
Ken Feduniewicz
Janice Cohen
Colorists

This one's for you, Mom and Dad. Thanks!

FIRST
GRAPHIC NOVEL

Teenage Mutant Ninja Turtles®
First Graphic Novel Number Nine

Teenage Mutant Ninja Turtles® and © 1986 Mirage Studios.
Teenage Mutant Ninja Turtles® Graphic Novel © 1986 First Comics Inc.
under exclusive license from Mirage Studios.
Introduction © 1986 Stanley Wiater.

All rights reserved, including the right to reproduce this book or any
portion thereof in any form whatsoever. The stories, incidents, and
characters mentioned in this publication are entirely fictional. No actual
persons, living or dead, without satiric content, are intended or should be
inferred. Teenage Mutant Ninja Turtles®, Raphael,™ Leonardo,™
Michaelangelo,™ Donatello™ and all prominent characters featured in this
publication are trademarks of Mirage Studios.

Published by First Comics Inc.
435 N. LaSalle Street, Chicago, IL 60610

ISBN: 0-915419-09-2

First Printing: November, 1986
Second Printing: July, 1987
Third Printing: June, 1988
Fourth Printing: September, 1988
Fifth Printing: August, 1989

11 12 13 14 15 16 17 18 19 20

Printed in the United States of America.

Rick Obadiah, Publisher   Ron Fascitelli, Sales Director
Kathy Kotsivas, Operations Director   Michael McCormick, Art Director
Kurt Goldzung, Creative Director   Rich Markow, Traffic Manager
Laurel Fitch, Editor   Fred Schiller, Production Supervisor

INTRODUCTION

What hath turtles wrought?

I know we're not discussing just any run-of-the-stream variety amphibians. No, these are the **Teenage Mutant Ninja** four-of-a-kind **Turtles**, that crawled from the primordial ooze which constantly perks in the brains of their creators **Peter Laird** and **Kevin Eastman**.

It's a safe assumption that those of you who have just purchased this first (of hopefully a long series of) **TMNT** graphic novels already know the life histories of Leonardo, Michaelangelo, Donatello and Raphael. You also probably can appreciate the fact that before they appeared on the comic book scene, you could count the number of successful black & white comics on Donatello's left hand. Simply compare a recent issue of *Comic Buyers' Guide* with one of a few years back to see how black & white comics have EXPLODED since **TMNT**'s arrival in May 1984. (And without naming names, other fellows are busily cranking out spoofs and parodies of **TMNT** – a classic sign of success in case Eastman and Laird still have any doubts as to whether they have finally *arrived*.) There are now **TMNT** figurines, T-shirts, iron-ons, role-playing games, with more tie-ins to follow even as we speak. But none of this magic would have occured if these two guys hadn't gotten together a few years back and gone – as Kevin would so aptly phrase it – "a little goofy."

So allow me to tell you a little about the creators of **TMNT**.

If you've been lucky enough to meet them briefly at a signing or convention, then you've glimpsed that these two gentlemen are actually what they appear to be: gentle men. Not crazed space cadets, or pompous mercenary fools. Just two decent, ordinary looking guys, whose only bad habit is that they still pinch themselves every once in a while to make sure it isn't all a crazy dream. But this shouldn't be such a shock: fictional heroes and the personalities of their creators often have nothing in common.

I mean, **Stephen King** – who Kevin says is a major influence on his writing style – doesn't sleep in a coffin or go around dressed in a black cape. And to throw in a barely relevant reference to *Star Trek* – one of Pete's biggest influences – **Gene Roddenberry** once told me, "Sure, I created *Star Trek* and all the characters. But that doesn't mean I sleep in Captain Kirk pajamas at night." (This also means if you want to impress Pete when you see him in the flesh, don't quote chapter and verse from **TMNT** or *Fugitoid*. If you *really* want to make him a buddy for life, come up with a model dinosaur for his private collection. Which one? For Peter, the only dinosaur he's truly obsessed with is the great three-horned beastie he's since transformed into a new species of immortality as the "Triceraton." And for Kevin, all you have to do is mention that you're a close personal friend of **Richard Corben**…)

I do want to make it abundantly clear that Peter and Kevin truly deserve all the success and fame they're received since first creating the Turtles in the fall of 1983. And fortune – Pete and I used to have to wait until "dollar night" to afford the latest science fiction or fantasy film at the Calvin Theater across the street from his apartment. (Now he could probably rent out the whole place for the night and show nothing but Ray Harryhausen movies. Come to think of it, he probably will once Hollywood produces the first feature-length **TMNT** movie.) But it wasn't all that long ago when he literally had to choose between buying art supplies for the "studio" in that one room apartment or buying another box of macaroni and cheese for more literal sustenance. For him, the cliché of starving-artist-in-a-third-floor-walk-up wasn't a joke, it was how he paid his dues.

Of course, Kevin wasn't born with a silver spoon in his mouth, or with subsidy rights to the *Silver Surfer* either. Until **TMNT** took off, he was supporting himself with the glorious job of working in a restaurant kitchen. Eight years younger than his partner and collaborator, Kevin first "met" Peter when he found a copy of a locally produced comic book called *SCAT* while on a bus ride from

Amherst to Northampton in 1982. As fate would have it, the magazine contained some of Pete's drawings. To make fate and a long story short, they soon met and realized they had the same life-long influences – **Jack Kirby** and **Frank Miller** – and interests – theorectical survival as artists.

The point I'm trying to make is, like all "overnight successes," Kevin and Peter have worked their butts off to get where they are. I could go on detailing their individual and collaborative struggles, but the bottom line remains simply this: both of these guys had lifelong dreams, and they *never let go of the dream*. If they were allowed to speak here, I'm sure *that* would be their one piece of advice to anyone even remotely considering careers in the comic book industry or as artists and writers in general.

Nobody handed them anything for free, or gave them a grant or scholarship to pursue their goal of taking the Turtles from the kitchen table drawing board and making them into the most sought after alternative comics creation in the business. In fact, neither the colleges or art schools they attended gave them any encouragement whatsoever to become comic book artists. And I'm reasonably sure that their parents told them for years that, "Comic books are nice, but what are you going to do when you *grow up*, and have to live in the *real world*?"

Well, although Pete has married – and Kevin is about to – neither has "grown up." The artists, writers and filmmakers they loved as kids, not so long ago, are still alive and are still admired enormously by Kevin and Peter. Only this time, our guys happen to be "pros" instead of "fans." Yet that intense love and admiration remains the same, and they never hesitate to acknowledge their debts to those who preceeded them.

Just as important, however, neither has to concern himself any longer with what he's going to do to survive in "the real world." They have fearlessly pursued their dreams, and now the "real world" – the merchandisers and the licensing agents – are banging away at the door to Mirage Studios, pleading to be allowed to share in their wonderfully realized fantasies. (There's a thought. Even the name of their company – Mirage – harkens back to when Pete and Kevin must have thought their dream of producing comics was just that: an illusion which *seems* real, but doesn't actually exist.)

What hath turtles wrought?

We don't need to be experts on popular culture to figure out the answer, do we? It's happiness. Happiness and fun. Not just for the hundreds of thousands – and perhaps eventually millions – of **TMNT** fans, but also for the two young men who refused to accept the dull and soul-crushing concept of everyday "reality." Refused to accept that, if there's anything more open to derision than the comic book industry, it's someone who's life goal is to actively work and *succeed* in that industry. And perhaps to change it, to possibly even make it better. Not with coy "revelance," or preachy moralizing, but with a wry sense of humor, a respect for the classic tradition of good art and storytelling. Along with an innate understanding and sincere appreciation for the intelligence of their audience. Coupled with the special ability to take a dozen types of old wines, and ferment a new blend which surpasses all which has gone before.

Teenage. Mutant. Ninja. Turtles.

In other words, the two gentlemen named **Peter Laird** and **Kevin Eastman** (just to reverse the billing this time). They deserve everything they're going to get. And you and I are just lucky enough to be with them from the beginning as it continues to get better.

Stanely Wiater
Holyhoke, Massachusetts
September, 1986

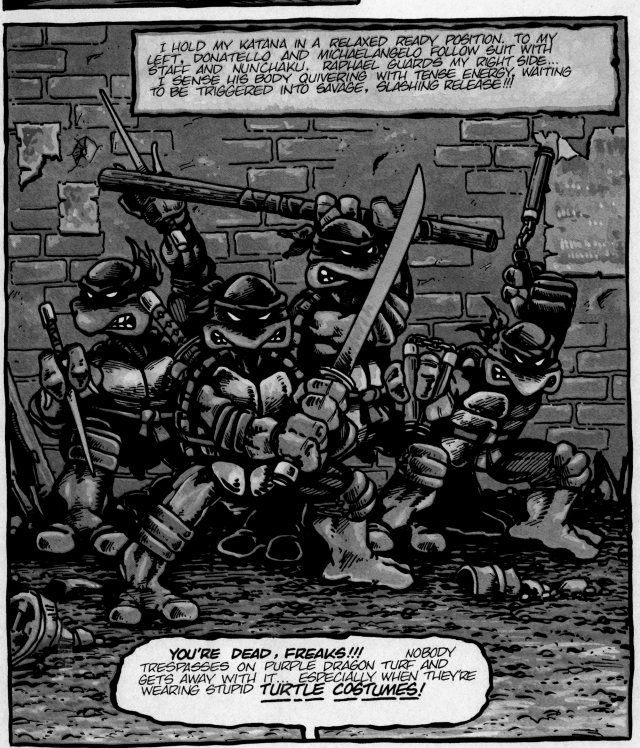

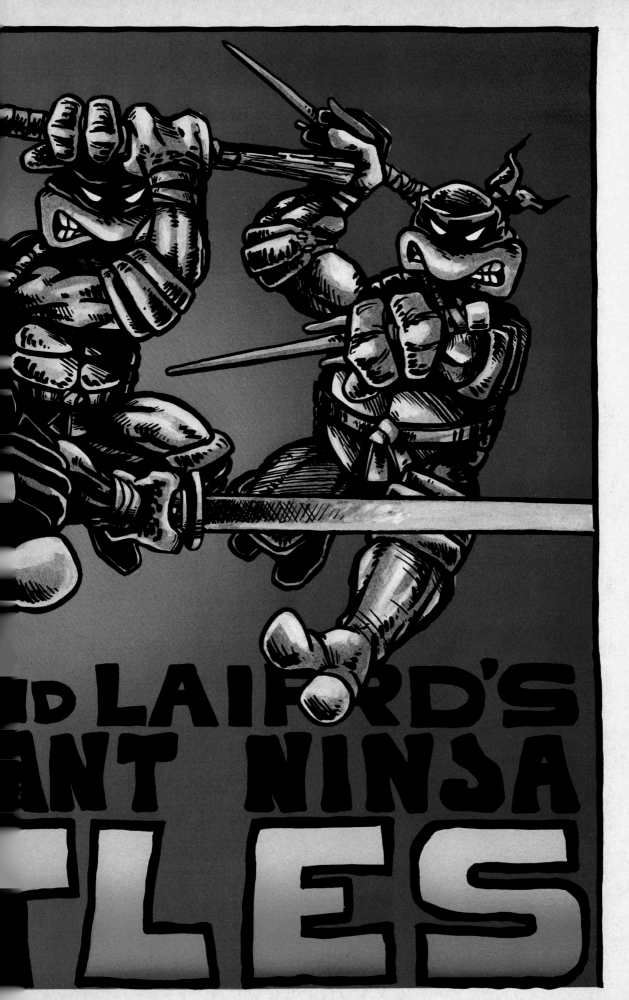

HEY!

HERE THEY COME! SCATTER!

THESE GUYS ARE YOUNG, BUT NO ROOKIES. THEY'VE BEEN AROUND, TOUGHENED BY THE STREETS. THEY'VE FOUGHT AND BEAT EVERYTHING ON TWO LEGS IN THIS AREA .... **EXCEPT US.**

WE HIT THEM AIRBORNE. I CUT TWO ON THE WAY DOWN. DONATELLO TAKES OUT A THIRD WITH HIS STAFF.

THE PUNKS DON'T WASTE MUCH TIME ON HAND-TO-HAND. THEY BREAK INTO SMALL GROUPS, AND OPEN UP WITH THEIR ARTILLERY!

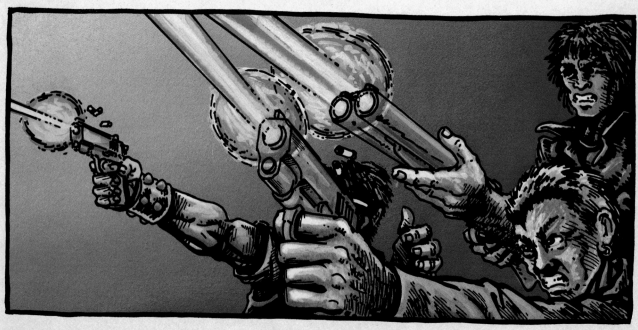

RAPHAEL LOVES THIS STUFF... THERE'S A FLASH AS HIS SAÏS COME OUT...

... THE THREE TOUGHS DON'T EVEN SEE THAT.

TOO BAD.

WHO ARE THESE GUYS--?

DON'T KNOW... SOME KINDA FREAKS!

BUT EVEN FREAKS CAN BLEED! CUT'EM!

YES, WE CAN BLEED...

... AND SO CAN YOU!

OUR FIRST MAJOR SKIRMISH IS OVER AND WE ARE STILL STANDING. OUR TRAINING HAS SERVED US WELL... **SPLINTER** WILL BE PLEASED.

A POLICE SIREN WAILS CLOSE BY, COMING FAST. WHEN THEY ARRIVE, THEY WILL FIND ONLY WHAT IS LEFT OF THE PURPLE DRAGON GANG.

WE DO NOT LIKE TO RUN FROM THOSE WHO WOULD BE OUR **ALLIES**, BUT THEY WOULD NOT UNDERSTAND US.

THE STORM DRAIN BECKONS. WE ARE NEVER FAR FROM A MEANS OF ESCAPE...

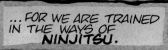

...FOR WE ARE TRAINED IN THE WAYS OF **NINJITSU.**

WE STRIKE **HARD** AND **FADE** AWAY...

...INTO THE NIGHT.

THE STORM DRAINS ARE OUR HOME. WE KNOW EVERY INCH OF THESE **SUBTERRANEAN PASSAGES.**

KLAK!

CREEEEEKKK!

FOR ALL OUR YEARS WE HAVE DWELT IN THESE **DARK DEPTHS...**

...LEARNING, GROWING AND BUILDING.

AH, MY SONS... YOU HAVE RETURNED AT LAST! YOU HAVE FOUGHT...?

AND WON, MASTER SPLINTER, AGAINST **FIFTEEN FOES!**

AH, YOU HAVE DONE WELL. YOUR SKILLS ARE AT THEIR **PEAK.**

I HAVE FORSEEN THIS NIGHT FOR MANY YEARS. NOW IT IS TIME...

...TIME FOR YOU TO BE TOLD OF THE MISSION FOR WHICH I HAVE TRAINED YOU THESE PAST **THIRTEEN YEARS.**

YOU WILL LEARN OF MY LIFE, AND HOW YOU CAME TO BE.

MY TALE BEGINS SOME **TWENTY YEARS AGO.**

I WAS A YOUNG RAT, A PET BOUGHT AND CARED FOR BY MY BELOVED MASTER, **HAMATO YOSHI.** MY CAGE WAS KEPT IN HIS DOJO, AND I WATCHED HIS DAILY PRACTICE. IT AMUSED HIM TO SEE ME MIMIC HIS MOVEMENTS...

BUT IT WAS MORE THAN MERE MIMICRY. SLOWLY I LEARNED HIS ART, **THE MYSTERIOUS MARTIAL ART OF NINJITSU.**

I COULD NOT HAVE HAD A BETTER TEACHER, FOR IT WAS SAID THAT HAMATO YOSHI WAS THE GREATEST SHADOW WARRIOR OF HIS CLAN.

HE WAS ONE OF THE FAMOUS "*FOOT*" CLAN, THE MOST FEARED WARRIORS AND ASSASSINS IN ALL JAPAN. ANOTHER MEMBER OF THE "*FOOT*" CLAN WAS *OROKU NAGI*. HE AND MY MASTER YOSHI COMPETED FIECELY IN ALL THINGS... ESPECIALLY FOR THE LOVE OF A YOUNG WOMEN, *TANG SHEN*.

BOTH TRIED TO WIN HER, BUT FROM THE START SHE LOVED ONLY ONE: MY MASTER, YOSHI.

 NAGI WAS INSANELY JEALOUS. ONE FATEFUL NIGHT, HE WENT TO SHEN TANG'S HOME AND **DEMANDED** THAT SHE LOVE HIM. SHEN REFUSED, SAYING THAT SHE WANTED ONLY YOSHI. IN A **JEALOUS RAGE**, NAGI BEGAN TO **BEAT** HER. AT THAT MOMENT YOSHI, HER LOVER, ENTERED THE ROOM AND SAW NAGI POISED TO **STRIKE !!!**

SHEN OH GODS... NO...!

HAH, **YOSHI DOG!** IF I CAN'T HAVE THIS **WENCH**.. THEN NO ONE WILL!

YOSHI'S WORLD VANISHED IN A **RED HAZE**...

...AND WHEN IT CLEARED, NAGI WAS NO MORE.

YOSHI'S SHAME WAS GREAT. BY KILLING ANOTHER MEMBER OF HIS CLAN, HE HAD DISHONORED HIMSELF. HIS CHOICES WERE SIMPLE, BUT NOT EASY: TO TAKE HIS OWN LIFE AND HOPE FOR HONOR IN THE NEXT LIFE; OR FLEE WITH SHEN TO ANOTHER COUNTRY AND TRY TO START LIFE AGAIN.

HE CHOSE THE LATTER, TAKING WITH HIM A FEW BELONGINGS, INCLUDING ME, AND CAME WITH SHEN TO **NEW YORK**. HERE MY MASTER FORMED A **MARTIAL ARTS SCHOOL**.

MEANWHILE, IN JAPAN...

NAGI...

...NAGI'S FAMILY, ESPECIALLY HIS YOUNGER BROTHER **SAKI**, WERE MOURNING HIS DEATH. THE SEVEN YEAR OLD SAKI VOWED **VENGEANCE** ON YOSHI. THE **FOOT** TOOK HOLD OF SAKI'S ANGER AND USED IT TO BEND HIM TO THEIR OWN PURPOSES. SAKI BEGAN INTENSIVE TRAINING IN THE **NINJA'S ART**, AND SOON SURPASSED HIS TEACHERS. AS HE GREW OLDER, HIS HATRED OF YOSHI GREW **DEEP** AND **BITTER**.

OROKU SAKI, YOU HAVE PROVEN YOURSELF. THOUGH YOU ARE ONLY EIGHTEEN, YOU ARE OUR MOST **CUNNING ASSASSIN...**

...AND AN ABLE LEADER! THEREFORE, WE HAVE CHOSEN YOU TO GO TO THE U.S. AND HEAD THE **NEW YORK** BRANCH OF THE "**FOOT**!"

AT LAST! A CHANCE TO AVENGE MY BROTHER'S **DEATH!**

SAKI MOVED QUICKLY. WITHIN A YEAR HE HAD BUILT THE NEW YORK "**FOOT**" INTO A FORCE TO BE RECKONED WITH.

14

UNDER SAKI'S LEADERSHIP, THE FOOT WAS SOON INVOLVED IN MANY CRIMINAL ACTIVITIES: DRUG SMUGGLING, ARMS RUNNING... AND THEIR SPECIALTY **ASSASSINATION**. SAKI, NOW CALLED **"THE SHREDDER"**, WAS SUCCESSFUL, BUT NOT SATISFIED. IN HIS HEART BURNED HATRED FOR **HAMATO YOSHI** AND HIS WIFE, **TANG SHEN**.

ON A NIGHT NEARLY FIFTEEN YEARS AGO, SAKI FINALLY MADE HIS MOVE...

THE TIME IS RIGHT... I HAVE TRACKED THEM DOWN...

...FOR THE MURDERER OF MY BROTHER, THERE WILL BE NO **ESCAPE**!!!

MY MASTER YOSHI CAME HOME THAT EVENING, NEVER EXPECTING THAT HIS MOST **DANGEROUS ENEMY** WAS LYING IN **WAIT**! ENTERING THE APARTMENT, HIS GAZE FELL ON THE **STILL, SILENT** FORM OF HIS BELOVED **SHEN**.

THEN HE SAW HER **KILLER**.

GOOD LORD ;CHOKE; **WHO ARE YOU?!**

I AM **OROKU SAKI**!

OH NO...;

IN THE STRUGGLE MY CAGE WAS SMASHED. I WAS FREE... BUT MY MASTER WAS **DEAD.** IN MY GRIEF I WANDERED THE STREETS, LIVING OFF SCRAPS OF **GARBAGE.**

THEN ONE DAY WHILE I WAS SEARCHING A TRASH CAN FOR MY NEXT MEAL, I WITNESSED AN ACCIDENT. AN OLD BLIND MAN CROSSING THE STREET WAS ALMOST RUN DOWN BY A LARGE **TRUCK.**

SKREEEE....!!

AT THE LAST MOMENT A YOUNG MAN LEAPED AT THE BLIND MAN AND **KNOCKED** HIM OUT OF THE TRUCK'S WAY. AS THE TRUCK SCREECHED TO A JARRING STOP, A METAL CANISTER BOUNCED OUT OF THE BACK OF THE TRUCK AND STRUCK THE YOUNG MAN NEAR HIS **EYES.**

UNNOTICED BY THE CROWD, THE **STRANGE CANISTER** BOUNCED SEVERAL MORE TIMES, STRIKING AND SMASHING A GLASS JAR WHICH HELD FOUR SMALL **TURTLES...** YOU FOUR AS **INFANTS!!!**
YOU FELL INTO THE MANHOLE, FOLLOWED BY THE CANISTER. FORTUNATELY A PILE OF DEAD LEAVES AND PAPERS BROKE YOUR FALL. BUT THE CANISTER SMASHED OPEN, RELEASING A **GLOWING OOZE** WHICH COVERED YOUR BODIES AS YOU CRAWLED AROUND IN IT.

16

I FOLLOWED YOU DOWN INTO THE STORM DRAIN, AND, NOT KNOWING EXACTLY WHY, GATHERED YOU UP IN A COFFEE CAN. I TOOK YOU TO MY BURROW AND WASHED OFF AS MUCH OF THE **GOO** AS I COULD.

THE NEXT MORNING I AWOKE TO FIND THE CAN TIPPED OVER, AND THE FOUR OF YOU **DOUBLED IN SIZE!!!** SOMEHOW, THAT STRANGE **OOZE** HAD AFFECTED YOUR GROWTH. AS I LEARNED LATER IT HAD CHANGED ME ALSO... MAKING ME MORE **INTELLIGENT**, AND **LARGER!**

BUT I DIDN'T GROW AS FAST AS YOU DID. WITHIN A YEAR, YOU HAD REACHED YOUR CURRENT SIZE. YOU FOLLOWED ME EVERYWHERE I WENT, EXCEPT ABOVE GROUND... I COULD NOT RISK YOUR BEING DISCOVERED.

I WAS AMAZED AT HOW INTELLIGENT YOU SEEMED, BUT EVEN SO I WAS NOT PREPARED FOR WHAT ONE DAY...HAPPENED ONE DAY...

SPLIN-TER?

...ONE OF YOU ACTUALLY SAID A WORD... **MY NAME!!!**

MORE WORDS FOLLOWED AND SOON YOU **ALL** WERE SPEAKING!

AROUND THIS TIME, YOU STARTED TO STAND **UPRIGHT,** AND COPY MY MOVEMENTS...

17

I BEGAN TRAINING YOU THEN, TEACHING YOU ALL THAT I HAD LEARNED FROM WATCHING MASTER YOSHI. I TAUGHT YOU THE USE OF WEAPONS, THE ART OF STEALTH, AND ALL THAT I KNEW OF THIS WORLD. IN TIME YOU SURPASSED MY LESSONS, AND BECAME TRUE **NINJA**. USING A BATTERED COPY OF A BOOK ON RENAISSANCE ART THAT I HAD FISHED OUT OF THE STORM DRAIN, I CHOSE NAMES FOR EACH OF YOU:

LEONARDO,

MICHAELANGELO,

DONATELLO,

AND RAPHAEL.

NOW, I AM OLD, AND THERE IS A TASK THAT I WOULD HAVE YOU PERFORM BEFORE I LEAVE THIS LIFE. NOW, I MUST ASK YOU TO DO THAT WHICH NO BEING SHOULD ASK OF ANOTHER... I ASK YOU TO AVENGE THE CRUEL DEATH OF MY MASTER, HAMATO YOSHI, AND HIS WIFE TANG SHEN. I ASK YOU TO CHALLENGE AND KILL THE MURDERER OROKU SAKI... **THE SHREDDER!**

18

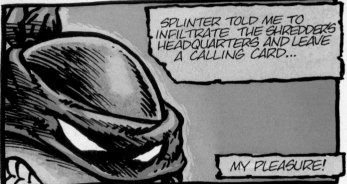

SPLINTER TOLD ME TO INFILTRATE THE SHREDDER'S HEADQUARTERS AND LEAVE A CALLING CARD...

MY PLEASURE!

TWO GUARDS ON THE RIGHT...

ONE ON THE FAR LEFT...

THEY'VE GOT TO GO.

THEY'LL BE MY CALLING CARD!

INTRUDER!

STOP HIM!!!

THEY'RE ARMED, OF COURSE...

THAT'S OK...

I AM, TOO.

HAII!

THE THIRD GUARD SEES THE ACTION, BUT DOESN'T SOUND THE ALARM...

...HE THINKS HE CAN TAKE ME OUT BY HIMSELF.

WHO ARE YOU?

NINJA?

TURTLE!

WE CONNECT IN MIDAIR...

...WHEN WE LAND, I'M **STANDING**...

...HE ISN'T.

NOW TO MY TASK!

THE MESSAGE IS WRAPPED AROUND ONE OF MY **SAIS**...

I CAN SEE **OROKU SAKI** INSIDE TALKING TO SOME **FLUNKIES**...

IT'S AN EASY SHOT!

SO YOU SEE, MR. McADAM, IT IS TO YOUR ADVANTAGE...

...TO HAVE MY **PROTECTION.**

22

HEY!

YAA!

GOOD LORD WHAT IS THAT!?

OROKU SAI... ALSO KNOWN AS THE... SHREDDER...

YOU HAVE SHAMED AND DISHONORED THE NAME OF YOUR FAMILY BY MURDERING HAMATO YOSHI. I GIVE YOU THE CHANCE TO REGAIN YOUR HONOR. MEET MY FOUR DISCIPLES FOR A DUEL TO THE DEATH TO-MORROW NIGHT AT THE FOLLOWING ADDRESS: H... 5TH STREET...

MR. OROKU, IS THIS THE PROTECTION YOU WOULD HAVE US PURCHASE? IF YOU CAN NOT KEEP YOUR OWN COMPLEX SECURE...

OUTRAGEOUS!

THEN WE CANNOT BELIEVE THAT YOUR PROTECTION IS WORTH ANYTHING!

GOODBYE, SIR!!

WHO CAN THIS CHALLENGE COME FROM? WHAT FOOL WOULD PIT HIS MINIONS AGAINST THE MIGHT OF THE SHREDDER?

IT DOESN'T MATTER... HIS EFFRONTERY WILL COME TO GRIEF SOON ENOUGH!

THERE WILL BE A DUEL, AND THERE WILL BE DEATH...

THEIRS!

THE FOLLOWING NIGHT...

ARBEE CONSTRUCTI[ON]

THIS IS IT, MY BROTHERS...

...USE YOUR CLIMBING CLAWS...

...AND GO SILENTLY!

SHREDDER, WE ARE HERE!

SHREDDER...
FACE US !!!

WHO ARE
THESE
FOOLS ?

26

THESE GUYS ARE GOOD!

ARRG! TOO GOOD!

BUT WE...

...ARE...

...BETTER!

30

31

BUT THAT WAS JUST STUDENTS FIGHTING STUDENTS; NOW YOU MUST FACE A **TEACHER.** A **MASTER !!!**

COME... ONE AT A TIME OR ALL AT ONCE, I DON'T CARE. FOR ONLY I WILL LEAVE HERE **ALIVE!**

ME FIRST !!!

YAAG!

SHAK!

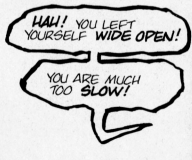

HAH! YOU LEFT YOURSELF **WIDE OPEN!**

YOU ARE MUCH TOO **SLOW!**

ARRG!

AMATEURS!!!

COME, GAIJIN... YOUR BROTHERS HAVE FALLEN! YOU ARE NEXT!

YAAA!

UNGH!

BAH... FOUR FOOLS!

HE IS **TOO SKILLED** FOR US TO FIGHT **ONE ON ONE**, BROTHERS! USE GROUP TACTICS... AND HIT FROM A **DISTANCE!!!**

UNN!

THUNK!

AGH! THUP!

36

NOW... YOU ARE **BEATEN**.

SO... FINISH... IT **FOOLS!** I AM... HELPLESS... SLAY ME **NOW!!!**

WE TURTLES ARE NOT DOGS WITHOUT HONOR...

...UNLIKE YOU, **OROKU SAKI.**

I WILL GIVE YOU ONE MORE CHANCE TO **REDEEM** YOUR **HONOR.**

TAKE THIS **KATANA**... AND COMMIT **SEPPUKU!**

NEVER!

IF... I MUST... KILL MYSELF... I WILL... TAKE... ALL OF YOU... TURTLES... WITH ME!

THIS... **THERMITE** GRENADE... WILL WIPE... THIS ROOF-TOP CLEAN OF ALL LIFE... INCLUDING YOU!!!

39

42

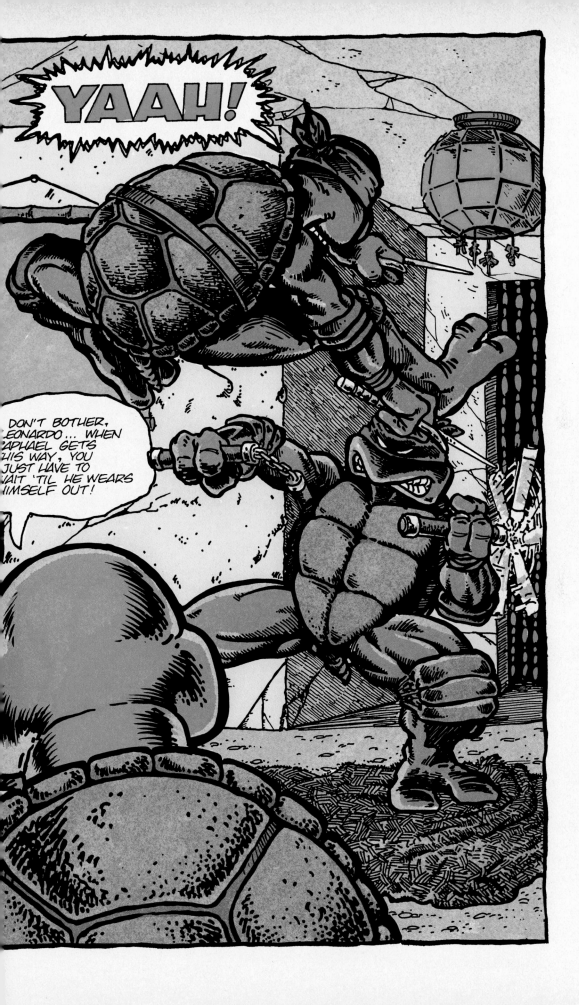

...AND MICHAELANGELO'S ALMOST AS BAD!

CRASH!

HMM, VERY BAD...

WHAT IS?

THIS NEWS PROGRAM... LISTEN, LEONARDO...

SO, DR. BAXTER STOCKMAN, YOU BELIEVE THAT THIS LITTLE... THING WILL SOLVE THE CITY'S RODENT PROBLEM?

THIS "LITTLE THING", MS. HYNES, IS A FULLY OPERATIONAL RODENT HUNTER/ SEEKER/ KILLER... WE LIKE TO REFER TO IT AS A "MOUSER"!

AS YOU CAN SEE, WE HAVE CONSTUCTED THIS MAZE TO SIMULATE THE CONDITIONS UNDER WHICH THE MOUSER WILL OPERATE.

NOW MY ASSISTANT APRIL WILL RELEASE FIVE RATS INTO THE MAZE...

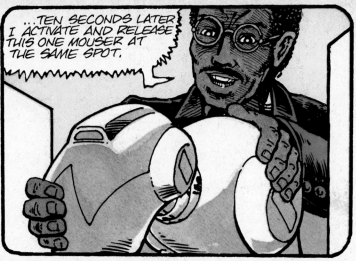

...TEN SECONDS LATER I ACTIVATE AND RELEASE THIS ONE MOUSER AT THE SAME SPOT.

THE MOUSER UNIT IS NOT IN ITSELF A VERY INTELLIGENT MACHINE...

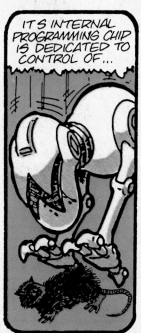

IT'S INTERNAL PROGRAMMING CHIP IS DEDICATED TO CONTROL OF...

...MOTIVE FUNCTIONING. A LARGER CENTRAL "MOTHER"...

...COMPUTER COORDINATES ALL SEARCH AND RETRIEVAL FUNCTIONS...

...AND WHEN IT'S WORK IS DONE, OR WHEN ITS STORGE CAPACITY OF FIVE AVERAGE-SIZED RATS IS FILLED, EACH MOUSER UNIT RETURNS TO A PREASSIGNED "DROP" POINT DIRECTED BY A REMOTE "MOTHER" UNIT.

SMASH!!!

OH NO, NOT ANOTHER PIECE OF FURNITURE?

SIGH...

MASTER, WHAT ABOUT THIS DR. STOCKMAN'S MOUSER?

WE MUST BE MORE CAUTIOUS FROM NOW ON, FOR ONE THING. HMM... LET ME THINK ON THIS A BIT!

I AM GOING TO MEDITATE. OH, AND RAPHAEL...

HELP MICHAELANGELO CLEAN UP THIS MESS!

SEVERAL WEEKS PASS... MANY RATS ARE CAUGHT BY DR. STOCKMAN'S "MOUSERS" ...BUT THE CITY ALSO EXPERIENCES A RASH OF BIZARRE BANK ROBBERIES.

LISTEN TO THIS BAXTER...

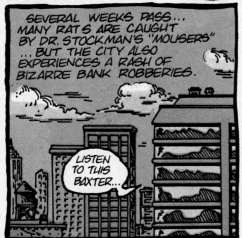

...IT SAYS THAT THE POLICE WERE BAFFLED BY THESE BANK HEISTS...

...THEY CAN'T FIGURE OUT HOW THE VAULTS WERE TUNNELED INTO SO SWIFTLY AND NEATLY, THROUGH CONCRETE AND STEEL!

THE TUNNELS WERE SO NARROW ONLY A CHILD COULD HAVE CRAWLED THROUGH THEM!

...OR A VERY SMALL ADULT. APRIL, WHY ARE YOU BORING ME WITH THIS?

WELL, IT'S JUST THAT I'VE BEEN THINKING...

THE MOUSER UNIT... THEY COULD HAVE DUG TUNNELS LIKE THAT, EASILY...

YES?

OH, COME NOW APRIL... WHY WOULD THE MOUSERS DIG HOLES IN BANK VAULTS? YOU HELPED PROGRAM THEM, REMEMBER?

BUT WHAT IF SOMEONE ELSE HAS GOTTEN CONTROL OF A COUPLE MOUSERS, AND REPROGRAMED THEM?

THE DAILY LUMPLE

REALLY APRIL... THE MOTHER COMPUTER WOULD KNOW IF THAT HAPPENED, AND WOULD TELL ME!

I... I SUPPOSE YOU'RE RIGHT, BAXTER... STILL, I...

THE DAILY LUMP

APRIL, I ASSURE YOU THAT NO ONE ELSE HAS CONTROL OVER THE MOUSERS EXCEPT YOU AND I.

COME ON... I HAVE SOMETHING TO SHOW YOU.

I'VE SEEN THE ELEVATOR BEFORE...

HA, HA, HA! NO, THIS IS DIFFERENT.

WHAT'S THAT, BAXTER?

YOU'LL SEE!

EMER-GENCY

HEY, WHAT'S GOING ON!?

SHHH...

48

WHERE DID YOU GET ALL OF THESE MOUSERS? THE CITY ONLY GAVE US ENOUGH FUNDS FOR *TWO DOZEN*...!

...AND THERE ARE MORE THAN TWO HUNDRED IN THIS ROOM! STILL MORE ARE BEING ASSEMBLED AS WE SPEAK!

TIC TIC CHIT

BUT BAXTER, HOW DID YOU GET THE MONEY...

OH, NO...!

VERY GOOD, APRIL, VERY PERCEPTIVE. I WOULD HAVE BEEN DISAPPOINTED AT ANYTHING LESS.

YES, THOSE RECENT BAFFLING BANK ROBBERIES ARE MY DOING!

WITH THE AID OF MY MOUSERS, I HAVE ALREADY STOLEN OVER $900,000!

OF COURSE, THAT IS ONLY THE BEGINNING. AT THIS MOMENT, HUNDREDS OF MOUSERS ARE TUNNELING THROUGHOUT THE CITY, UNDERMINING AND WEAKENING THE FOUNDATIONS OF CERTAIN LARGE AND IMPORTANT BUILDINGS!

WHEN THEY ARE NEARLY DONE, I'LL HOLD THE CITY FOR *RANSOM*... AND IF I'M REFUSED, I WILL ORDER MY MOUSERS TO FINISH THE *EXCAVATION*... AND THOSE BUILDINGS WILL FALL!

BUT-- WHY?

WHY, BAXTER? YOU COULD MAKE MILLIONS LEGALLY!

50

YOU'RE QUITE RIGHT, APRIL... THE MONEY IS ONLY AN INCIDENTAL...... A BY-PRODUCT.

I'M REALLY DOING IT BECAUSE IT'S *FUN!!* HAH, HAH, HA HAH!

I DON'T BELIEVE WHAT I'M HEARING! THIS JUST ISN'T THE DR. STOCKMAN I'VE WORKED WITH ALL THIS TIME!

HA, HA, HA HAH, HAH!

HE'S IN HIS OWN WORLD RIGHT NOW... I'D BETTER MAKE A RUN FOR IT WHILE I CAN!

WELL IF YOU WANT TO BE THAT WAY, THEN *GO!* I DON'T NEED YOU!

I DON'T NEED ANYONE EXCEPT MY *MOUSERS!*

I SUPPOSE YOU'RE GOING TO RUSH OFF AND TELL THE *POLICE* ABOUT ME AND MY PLAN...

SIGH... ONE MUST DO WHAT ONE MUST DO, I GUESS.

OH, WAIT... I NEED THAT I.D. CARD TO WORK THE ELEVATOR...

BAXTER, WAIT!

SLAM!

NOOOO!

SORRY APRIL...

YOU MUST REALIZE I WON'T... CAN'T... HELP YOU TURN ME IN...

SO I'M MAKING IT A LITTLE MORE DIFFICULT FOR YOU TO LEAVE, BUT NOT IMPOSSIBLE. WATCH YOUR STEP!

HA, HA, HA!

DRAMATIC HUH? SORRY ABOUT THE...

...MUCKY WATER, BUT IT COLLECTS THERE AFTER IT RAINS!

AT LEAST IT ISN'T OVER YOUR HEAD!

BAXTER, YOU SLIME PUPPY!

WELL I'M NOT GOING TO STAY HERE IN THIS **FOUL SMELLING HOLE,** AND THIS TUNNEL LOOKS LIKE THE ONLY WAY OUT!

YUCK! I HOPE THIS TUNNEL ENDS SOON...

HMM... IT LOOKS LIKE IT OPENS INTO A LARGER TUNNEL UP AHEAD!

NOW WHERE DO I GO FROM HERE?

IT REALLY DOESN'T MATTER

TRICKING YOU INTO THE STORMDRAIN TUNNELS HAS GIVEN ME THE TIME TO PROGRAM YOUR IMMINENT DEMISE...

HMM... HOW MANY SHOULD I SEND AFTER HER?

THREE? FIVE? TEN, MAYBE? NO... THREE WILL BE **PLENTY!**

HA, HA, HA! WHAT DELIGHTFUL IRONY! SLAIN BY THE VERY TECHNOLOGICAL MARVELS WHICH HER COMPUTER SKILLS MADE POSSIBLE!

"I'VE GIVEN THEM ENOUGH DATA TO TRACK HER DOWN...

"...HER SIZE, SCENT, HER VOICE PRINT... *GOODBYE* APRIL!"

HA HA HA HAH

MEANWHILE...

IT'S SO DARK AND CREEPY IN HERE!

I HOPE I FIND A LADDER SOON!

EH?

WHAT'S THAT NOISE?!

OH, NO....!

THE MOUSERS!!! THAT TWISTED BAXTER! HE'S TRYING TO *KILL* ME!!!

GOT TO RUN!

GOTTA GET AWAY FROM THEM!

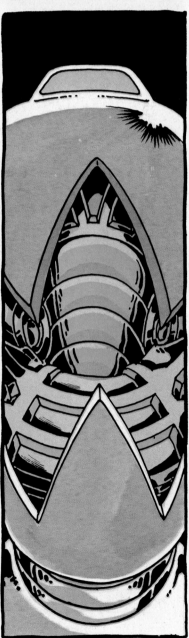

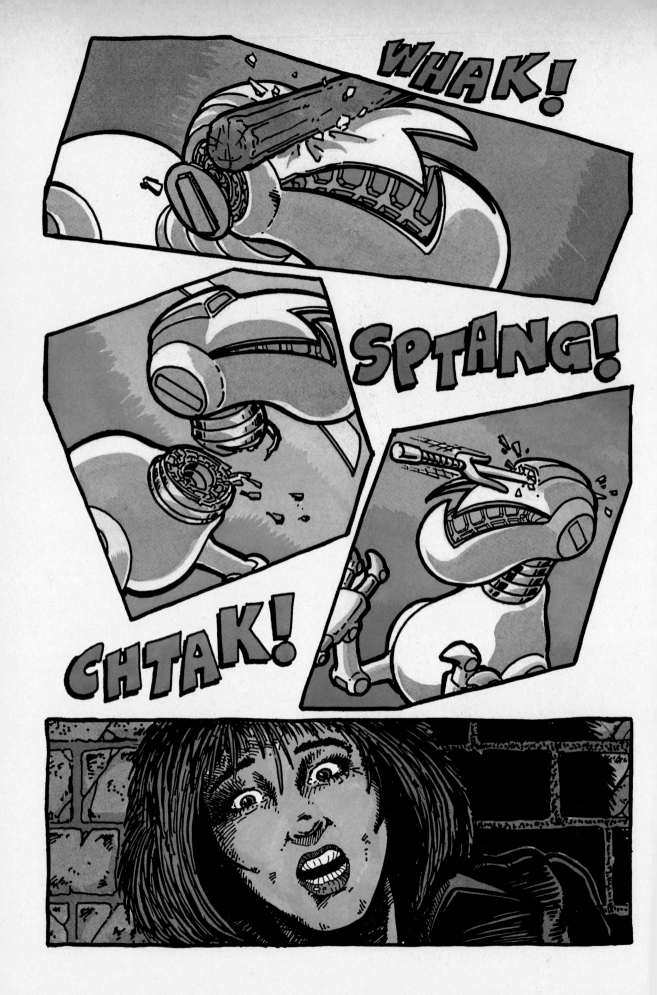

56

I CAN'T...

DEAL WITH...

THISSSS ⁎

LATER...

...FAINTED, SPLINTER. THEN WE CARRIED HER, AND THE REMAINS OF THOSE THREE "MOUSERS", BACK HERE!

HMMM... I SUPPOSE YOUR UNEXPECTED APPEARANCE WAS QUITE A SHOCK TO HER SYSTEM.

OF COURSE, BEING CHASED THROUGH DARK TUNNELS BY A PACK OF **BLOOD THIRSTY ROBOTS** PROBABLY DIDN'T HELP...

SHE'S WAKING UP!

OHHH...

OHH!! SO... ...SO... YOU ARE REAL! I WASN'T IMAGINING YOU! WHERE AM I?

YOU ARE SAFE, YOUNG WOMAN...

58

...SAFE IN OUR HOME.

WH...WHO...?

MY NAME IS **SPLINTER,** AND YES. I AM A RAT. I AM ALSO THE TEACHER OF THESE TURTLES WHO RESCUED YOU...

...LEONARDO...

...DONATELLO...

...AND RAPHAEL!

THERE IS ALSO **MICHAELANGELO,** WHO WAS HERE AT HOME.

HI!

WELL... THANK YOU ALL FOR SAVING ME FROM THOSE ROBOTS. UH... JUST WHAT ARE YOU, AND WHERE DID YOU COME FROM, IF YOU DON'T MIND ME ASKING...?

NOT AT ALL! OURS IS A LONG STORY, THOUGH...

ONE HOUR LATER...

WHAT A FANTASTIC STORY!

NOW THAT YOU'VE AVENGED YOUR MASTER AND DEFEATED THE SHREDDER... WHAT WILL YOU DO? WHAT PURPOSE WILL INSPIRE YOUR LIVES NOW?

THAT IS A VERY GOOD QUESTION, APRIL. IT DEPENDS MOSTLY ON WHAT MY STUDENTS...

MASTER SPLINTER! COME QUICK... THERE'S SOMETHING ON THE T.V. YOU SHOULD SEE!

...POLICE AND FIRE DEPARTMENTS HAVE EVACUATED THE BUILDING...

... AND CLEARED THE AREA AROUND IT, IN CASE THE BUILDING IN FACT DOES FALL, AS THE MYSTERIOUS TERRORIST HAS THREATENED.

HERE AGAIN IS THE VIDEO-TAPED "RANSOM" NOTE DELIVERED TO CITY HALL JUST ONE HOUR AGO:

MY GOD... THAT'S BAXTER!

GREETINGS CITIZENS OF NEW YORK.

WHO I AM IS NOT IM-PORTANT...

...WELL, NOT AS IMPORTANT AS WHAT I AM PREPARED TO DO!

I INTEND TO EXTORT ONE BILLION DOLLARS FROM THE MAJOR BUSINESSES OF NEW YORK CITY!

HOW DO I INTEND TO DO THIS, YOU SAY?

SIMPLE! BY SYSTEMATICALLY HOLDING HOSTAGE EVERY CORPORATE HEADQUARTERS BUILDING IN THIS CITY!

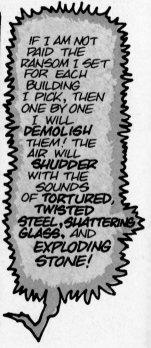

IF I AM NOT PAID THE RANSOM I SET FOR EACH BUILDING I PICK, THEN ONE BY ONE I WILL DEMOLISH THEM! THE AIR WILL SHUDDER WITH THE SOUNDS OF TORTURED, TWISTED STEEL, SHATTERING GLASS, AND EXPLODING STONE!

NOW JUST TO SHOW THAT I AM NOT JESTING... AND TO SHOW THAT I'M NOT A CHEAP KIND OF GUY... I'M GOING TO GIVE YOU A **FREEBIE**!

I HAVE IN MY HAND A SMALL MODEL OF THE **RETXAB** BUILDING...

...ITS REAL LIFE COUNTERPART IN DOWNTOWN MANHATTAN (VACANT EXCEPT FOR A FEW SMALL OFFICES SINCE THE PREVIOUS OWNERS VANISHED MYSTERIOUSLY) WILL CEASE TO EXIST AT 3:00 PM TODAY!

... AND TOMORROW, AT 3:00 PM...

ONE OF THE WORLD TRADE CENTER TOWERS WILL TOPPLE... ... UNLESS I AM PAID **20 MILLION DOLLARS**!

THE UNIDENTIFED TERRORIST THEN WENT ON TO DESCRIBE A COMPLEX ARRANGEMENT FOR DELIVERY OF THE RANSOM MONEY.

HOWEVER, IT HAS NOT BEEN DETERMINED IF THIS THREAT IS FOR REAL OR MERELY PART OF AN ELABORATE HOAX; AS YOU CAN SEE, IT IS NOW 3:03 PM AND THE **RETXAB** BUILDING IS STILL STANDING.

SO I GUESS THIS WILL WRAP IT... HUH?

GOOD LORD!

≥CHOKE≤

OH MY GOD... BAXTER... NOOO!

JONIN SPLINTER... THIS MAN IS MAD! HE MUST BE STOPPED!

≥SOB≤

APRIL... DO YOU THINK YOU CAN FIND YOUR WAY BACK TO BAXTER'S SECRET LAB?

I... I... THINK... ...SO...

"THEN GO WITH HER, MY NINJA... AND USE YOUR EVERY SKILL TO QUENCH THIS MADNESS!"

LATER...

MARVELOUS...!

THIS IS GREAT!

I THINK I'LL RUN THOSE TAPES AGAIN!

CREAK!

YOUR REIGN OF TERROR HAS ENDED, STOCKMAN!

EH?

W--WHAT! WHO ARE YOU?

H-HOW DID YOU GET IN HERE?

THEY CAME WITH ME, BAXTER...

...TO HELP STOP YOUR SCHEMES!

APRIL! YOU'RE STILL ALIVE!

DON'T MOVE ANOTHER INCH, BUCKO!

NO THANKS TO YOU, CREEP! YOUR MOUSERS WOULD HAVE KILLED HER IF NOT FOR US!

NOOO...

NOW, LET'S SEE... I'M SURE I CAN FIGURE OUT HOW TO SHUT THIS SYSTEM DOWN...

I'LL TRY THIS-- UGH!

CR EAK!

YOW!

RUMBLE!

POP

THE WHOLE SHAFT IS **JAMMED** WITH **ROCKS!** ANOTHER BIT OF STOCKMAN'S BLASTED PLAN!

OH MY GOD... WE'RE TRAPPED! THERE'S NOTHING WE CAN DO!!!

WAIT A MINUTE, APRIL! I'M FAMILIAR WITH SOME COMPUTER SYSTEMS... AND YOU HELPED PROGRAM THE **MOUSERS.** MAYBE WE CAN DO SOMETHING TO CANCEL THIS **DESTRUCT PROGRAM!**

I SUPPOSE IT'S POSSIBLE, DONATELLO...

...BUT IT WOULD TAKE **TIME** -- AND THOSE MOUSERS WILL BE HERE **SOON!**

I'VE GOT A PLAN THAT MIGHT DELAY THEM, APRIL!

IF BAXTER KEPT ANY **EXPLOSIVES** HERE...

HEY, LEO... I THINK I'VE GOT WHAT YOU NEED HERE!

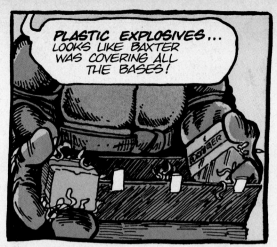

PLASTIC EXPLOSIVES... LOOKS LIKE BAXTER WAS COVERING ALL THE BASES!

GREAT, RAPHAEL-- THESE LITTLE BABIES SHOULD BUY US SOME TIME!

OPEN THE DOORS TO THE TUNNELS!

SNIK

WHAT? ARE YOU CRAZY!

DO IT!

I THINK I KNOW WHAT HIS PLAN IS, RAPHAEL...

YOU'RE GOING TO BLOW THE TUNNEL, RIGHT?

YOU GOT IT!

PUT THEM HERE... ABOUT 30 YARDS FROM THE LAB! WHEN THESE SUPPORTS GO, THE TUNNEL WILL COLLAPSE AT THIS POINT... THAT SHOULD SLOW THEM DOWN A LITTLE!

THERE... ALL DONE!

O.K. ...LIGHT 'EM UP!

UT-OH...

CHIT SCRATCH TIC TIC TIC CHITTER SCR

68

NO GOOD! NOT ENOUGH TIME... IT WOULD TAKE DAYS TO WRITE A VIRUS PROGRAM... WE'VE GOT MINUTES!

BLAST!

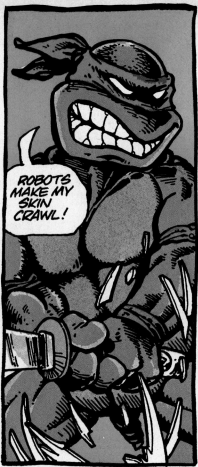

ROBOTS MAKE MY SKIN CRAWL!

WAIT A MINUTE! HOW ARE THE MOUSERS, CONTROLLED... BY RADIO?

WHY, YES- THE COMPUTER'S INSTRUCTIONS ARE BEAMED TO EACH UNIT'S RADIO RECEIVER!

IF WE CAN SOME HOW SHUT DOWN ALL THE POWER, THE TRANSMITTER HERE WILL STOP BROAD-CASTING THE, COMPUTER'S ORDERS TO THE MOUSERS!

ASSUMING OF COURSE THAT THE TRANSMITTER IS PART OF THIS SYSTEM!

WE'VE GOT TO TRY IT!

WAIT...! I THINK I HAVE SOMETHING HERE!

IT LOOKS LIKE AN EMERGENCY SHUT DOWN PROGRAM!

IT MIGHT WORK!

76

TIC TIC CRASH SMASH CHIT CHITTER BLANG
CHIT ZHRROOUUNNNN
CHIT CHITTER CHITTER CRASH TIC TIC CHIT

HAI THUMP BANG CHITTER
CHIT CHITTER CRASH TIC
TINKLE TINKLE! CHIT TIC

CHIT
SLASH THUMP THU-WACK
CHIT CHITTER

HEY...

Eastman & Laird's
TEENAGE MUTANT NINJA
TURTLES

ONCE THE POLICE FIND OUT THAT BAXTER WAS BEHIND ALL THAT CRAZINESS, I -- AS HIS EX-ASSISTANT -- WILL HAVE TO ANSWER SOME QUESTIONS!

BUT I'M MORE WORRIED ABOUT YOU GUYS -- PRETTY SOON YOUR TUNNELS WILL BE CRAWLING WITH COPS AND REPAIR CREWS. YOU'VE GOT TO FIND A BETTER PLACE TO HIDE-OUT!

YOU'RE RIGHT -- I'M SURE MASTER SPLINTER WILL KNOW WHAT TO DO!

WELL... I WISH YOU WELL. HERE'S MY PHONE NUMBER... IF YOU NEED MY HELP, PLEASE CALL!

THANKS, APRIL -- WE WILL!

LATER...

UH, OH -- I DON'T LIKE THE LOOK OF THIS --

OUR HOME --

-- IT'S BEEN BROKEN INTO!

CREEK!

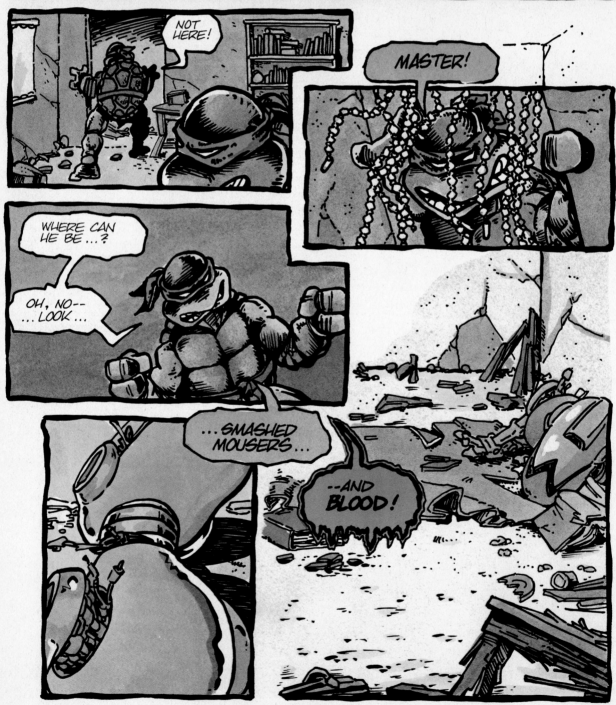

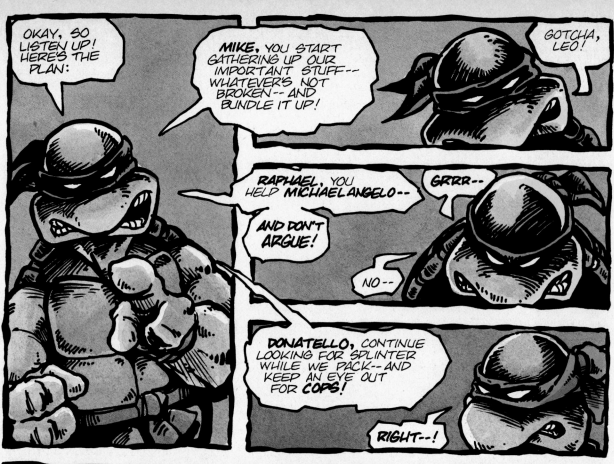

OKAY, SO LISTEN UP! HERE'S THE PLAN:

MIKE, YOU START GATHERING UP OUR IMPORTANT STUFF-- WHATEVER'S NOT BROKEN-- AND BUNDLE IT UP!

GOTCHA, LEO!

RAPHAEL, YOU HELP MICHAELANGELO--

GRRR--

AND DON'T ARGUE!

NO--

DONATELLO, CONTINUE LOOKING FOR SPLINTER WHILE WE PACK-- AND KEEP AN EYE OUT FOR COPS!

RIGHT--!

--IM GOIN' TO LOOK FOR SPLINTER!

RAPHAEL WAIT!!!

BLAST IT! RAPHAEL, YOU BE BACK HERE IN TEN MINUTES!

THAT RAPHAEL HAS SUCH A SHORT FUSE!

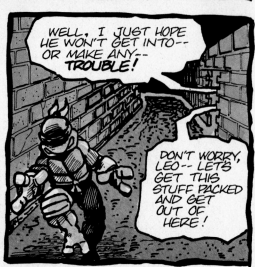

WELL, I JUST HOPE HE WON'T GET INTO-- OR MAKE ANY-- TROUBLE!

DON'T WORRY, LEO-- LET'S GET THIS STUFF PACKED AND GET OUT OF HERE!

LATER...

WHERE IS HE!? I KNEW HE'D DO SOMETHING LIKE THIS--!

RAPHAEL COULD BE IN A REAL JAM, LEO-- THE PLACE WAS OVERRUN WITH COPS AND WORKMEN!

WE BARELY MADE IT OUT OURSELVES!

WELL, DANGEROUS OR NOT, WE'VE GOT TO GO BACK AND FIND HIM!

NO NEED, GUYS-- I'M BACK!

RAPHAEL!

YOU DIDN'T HAVE TO WORRY-- I HAD NO PROBLEM GETTING AWAY!

RAPHAEL, DON'T YOU EVER DO THAT AGAIN-- EVER !!!

WE HAVE TO STICK TOGETHER, LIKE SPLINTER TAUGHT US!

I KNOW, I KNOW-- I'M SORRY! BUT I HAD TO LOOK FOR SPLINTER! NO SIGN OF HIM, THOUGH!

WE'LL ALL LOOK FOR HIM LATER, RAPH -- BUT NOW OUR NEXT MOVE IS TO CALL APRIL, AND SEE IF SHE CAN HIDE US!

85

HEY, THERE'S APRIL!

THAT WAS FAST!

BEEP BEEP

SKREE

OKAY, LET'S GO!

JUMP IN, GUYS!

ALL ABOARD-- LET'S ROLL!

NEAT VAN!

YOU GOT IT, LEO! GOSH, IT'S GOOD TO SEE YOU ALL AGAIN. HEY-- WHERE'S SPLINTER?

SPLINTER WASN'T... I'M AFRAID... HE WASN'T AT HOME WHEN WE GOT THERE... THE PLACE WAS IN *SHAMBLES*... MOUSERS EVERYWHERE!

NO--!

VROOM CLICK RRRR

HE CAN'T BE-- GONE! HE CAN'T--!

WE DIDN'T FIND HIS BODY, SO THERE'S STILL HOPE. WE WANT TO GO LOOK FOR HIM AS SOON AS *POSSIBLE*.

ONCE WE GET YOU SETTLED AT MY PLACE, YOU CAN GO LOOK FOR HIM RIGHT AWAY--

--AND I'LL HELP YOU AS MUCH AS I CAN!

THANKS, APRIL!

YEAH!

VROOM

HEY--!

HUH?

88

89

MIKE! GRAB THE LICENSE PLATE OFF THE BACK OF THE VAN! IF WE'RE LUCKY THEY HAVEN'T TAKEN DOWN THE NUMBERS YET!

YA-HOO! THIS IS GREAT... JUST LIKE "HILL STREET"!

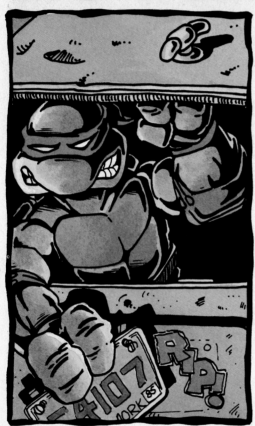

WHAT THE HELL WAS THAT!?

THESE GUYS WEARIN' MASKS OR SOMETHIN'?!

I'LL HEAD FOR THE BOULEVARD -- THE TRAFFIC'S HEAVY THERE, AND I CAN LOSE THEM!

IT'S JUST AROUND THE NEXT--

HEY-- THEY'RE MAKING A BREAK!

--AND WATCH OUT FOR PEDESTRIANS!

HEY-- I THINK I CAN TAKE OUT THEIR TIRES!

WHAT--?! DON'T SHOOT, YOU FOOL!

WHAT DO YOU THINK THIS IS, THE A-TEAM!!?

THERE ARE TOO MANY CITIZENS AROUND-- YOU'D PROBABLY HIT SOMEONE!

I PITY THE MAN!

MAYBE WE COULD JUMP FOR IT AND GET AWAY--!

I DON'T THINK APRIL'S QUITE UP TO OUR KIND OF ACROBATICS, RAPHAEL...

ISN'T IT A LOVELY NIGHT, DEAR?

HEAD FOR THAT BRIDGE, APRIL-- THEN LET'S GET OUT OF THIS PARK BEFORE WE RUN SOMEBODY OVER!

94

LEO, THIS IS AWFUL! THREE CARS WRECKED-- PEOPLE HURT!

I DON'T THINK THEY'RE HURT THAT SERIOUSLY, APRIL.

AND REMEMBER, THEY STARTED CHASING US-- AND WE DIDN'T DO ANYTHING WRONG!

I--GUESS YOU'RE RIGHT-- BUT WE'VE GOT TO STOP IT SOMEHOW--!

TRY THIS-- SWING AROUND THAT NEXT CAR AND GO UP THE FIRST RIGHT HAND SIDE STREET!

HEY, NICK--!

COPS! LOTS OF 'EM, AND COMIN' FAST!

DAMN! THEY MUST KNOW WE PULLED THAT ROBBERY!

DON'T PANIC, SLIM-- MAYBE THEY'RE CHASIN' SOMEBODY ELSE, LIKE THIS...

FASTER, APRIL! HEY, THERE'S A SIDE STREET-- TAKE A SHARP RIGHT!

WE WON'T MAKE IT!

...LIKE-- THIS OTHER-- VAN?

HEY WHA--?

EH!?

LEO, THAT VAN--

SO THIS IS YOUR HOME, APRIL? NICE!

THANKS, MIKE! LET ME GET OUT FIRST AND UNLOCK THE DOOR--

--AND LOOK AROUND--

581

--O.K.-- COAST IS CLEAR!

LET'S GO!

THIS WAY, GUYS-- --WATCH YOUR FEET!

LOTS OF JUNK IN HERE!

CRASH
TINKLE
TINKLE

OOPS!

MY APARTMENT'S THE ONLY ONE IN THE BUILDING THAT'S LIVEABLE RIGHT NOW--

--BUT TOMORROW YOU CAN CHECK OUT THE UPSTAIRS AND THE CELLAR, AND SEE WHAT YOU'D LIKE TO DO.

NO ONE ELSE LIVES HERE?

WELL, MY DAD USED TO LIVE HERE UNTIL HIS STROKE, ABOUT SIX MONTHS AGO. NOW HE LIVES IN A -- A, WELL A NURSING HOME ...

I'M SORRY... I ... THINK I KNOW HOW YOU FEEL.

OUR "FATHER" IS GONE, TOO.

BUT WE WILL FIND HIM!

THE END

NEW COMIC DAY... I LOVE IT!

HEY, DON-- GOT YOUR COPY OF AMERICAN SPLENDOR!

DON...? HUH... HE MUST BE OUT...

NICE NEW CHAIR HE'S GOT-- REAL COMFY! MAYBE I'LL JUST RELAX HERE A BIT...

...SHOPPING CAN REALLY :YAWN: TIRE A GUY OUT...

EH...?

WHUZZAT...?! EARTHQUAKE?!!

OWMPH!

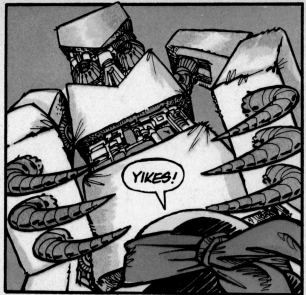

YIKES!

I'M *OUTA* HERE! ONE THING'S FOR SURE...

...THAT'S NO "*LAZ-E-BOY*"! BUT ENOUGH'S ENOUGH--!

NO STUFFED MONSTROSITY IS GONNA PUSH ME AROUND--

--EVEN IF IT IS *TASTEFULLY UPHOLSTERED!*

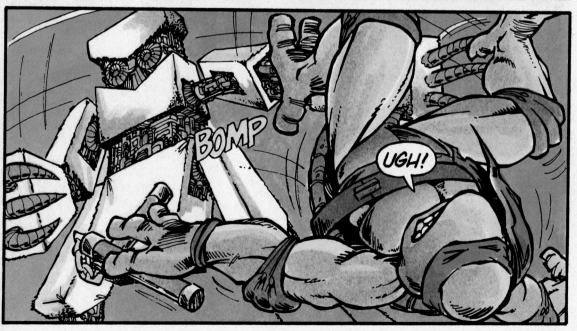

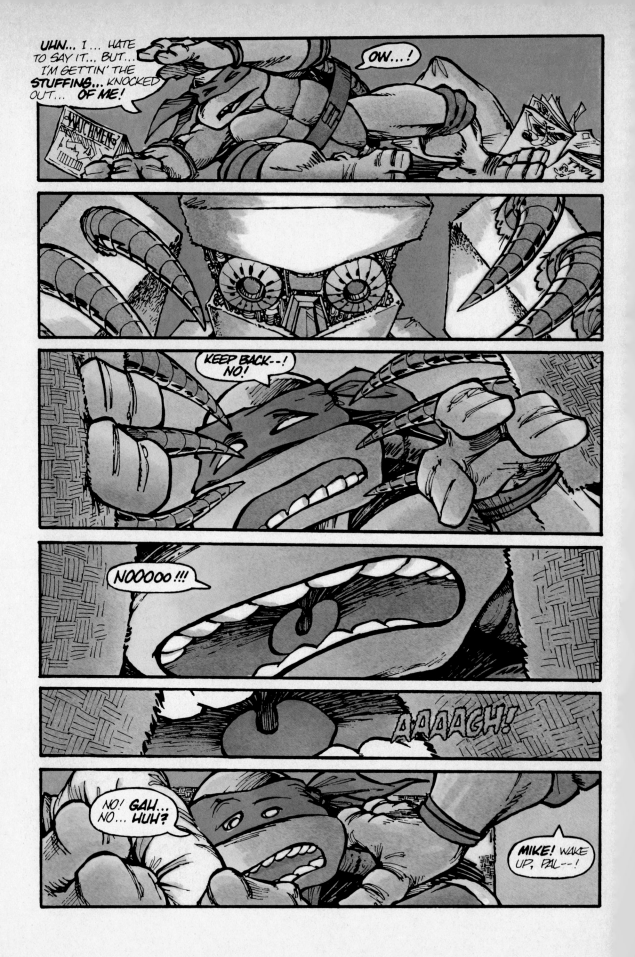

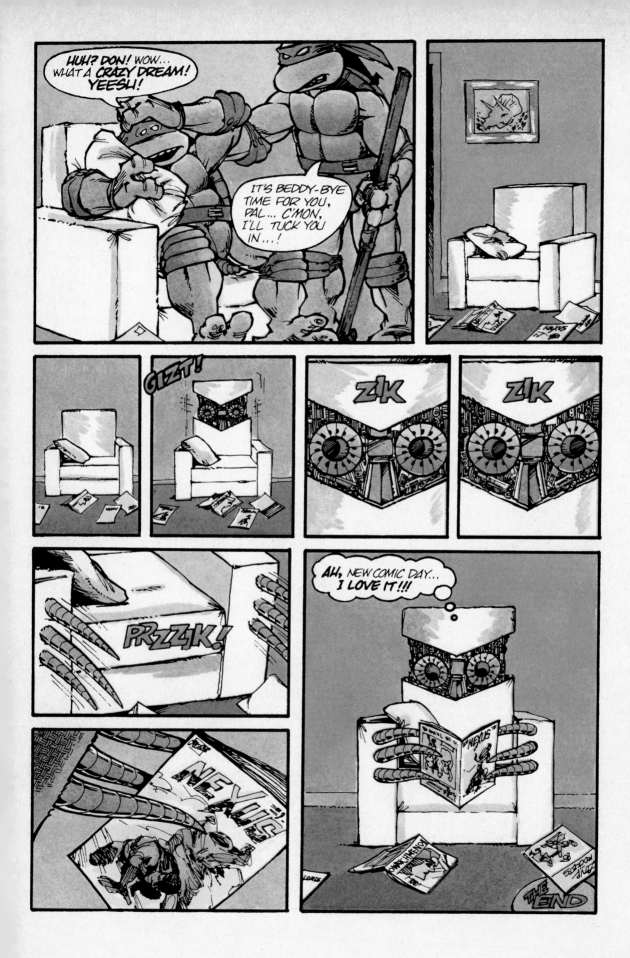

THE TEENAGE MUTANT NINJA TURTLES IN **NIGHT LIFE** STORY AND PENCILS - KEVIN EASTMAN INKS - RYAN BROWN LETTERS - STEVE LAVIGNE

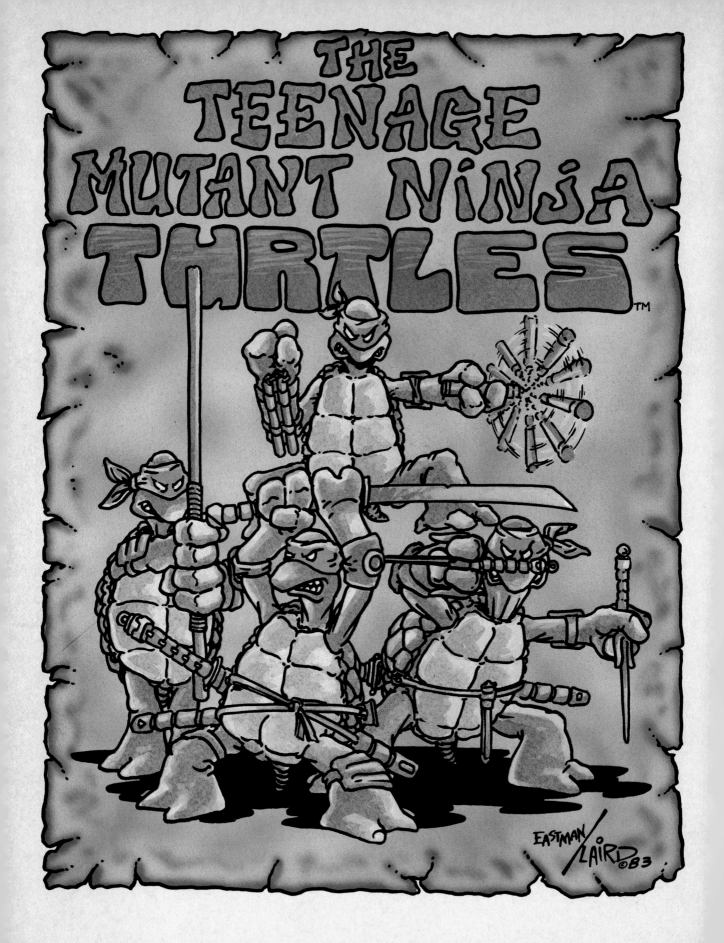

Kevin Eastman was born on May 30th, 1962 in Portland, Maine. After briefly attending Portland School of Art and the University of Southern Maine, he continued his artistic studies by freelance illustrating and attending classes at night.

After a year of writing and drawing stories for Clay Geerde's *Comix Wave* and Brad Foster's *Goodies,* he met Peter Laird in the fall of 1982. Discovering a mutual love for the art of graphic storytelling (and Jack Kirby), Peter and Kevin worked on a few small projects before founding the then Dover, New Hampshire based Mirage Studios in the fall of 1983.

It was there, just a few month later, while working on their first creation, *Fugitoid,* that Kevin drew a sketch that together they would shape into the characters contained in this book, **Teenage Mutant Ninja Turtles.**

Photo by Laurie Ganz

Peter Alan Laird was born in North Adams, Massachusetts on January 27, 1954. His love of drawing was evident at an early age, as was his fascination with dinosaurs, robots, and other things of an outré nature.

On his way to breaking into the comics field, Laird made several temporary digressions, including obtaining a Bachelor of Fine Arts degree in printmaking from the University of Massachusetts at Amherst; self-publishing an unabashedly bad *homage* to Barry Smith's *Conan* titled *Barbaric Fantasy;* contributing cartoons and illustrations to the UMASS student newspaper, the *Daily Collegian,* co-creating and contributing to a free monthly comic book call *Scat;* and making the archetypical "starving artist's" living as a freelance illustrator for about eight years.

It was a chance meeting with a young and prodigiously talented illustrator – Kevin Eastman – in Northampton in 1982 that started Laird on his current path, and which ultimately led to the much-sought-after "big break." Laird and Eastman's collaboration on their self-published **Teenage Mutant Ninja Turtles** comic book was – and is – very successful and rewarding, aesthetically and financially. Since November of 1984, when issue #2 of **TMNT** was being drawn, Laird has not looked for any outside freelance work, devoting himself entirely to the turtles.

Actually, Laird is at least as devoted to his wife, writer Jeannine Atkins, with whom he lives in Haydenville, MA.

Photo by Laurie Ganz

Steve *(Moondog)* **Lavigne** is believed to be a Maine native as he was spotted at several schools and recreational sites there. Steve kicked his way into the comics field by taking on lettering jobs from Mirage Studios in 1985. An artist in his own right, he was inspired to draw by the incredible Walt Disney animation department and later by comic books themselves. Steve was last seen in Northampton, Massachusetts, where he is refining his drawing and painting skills and plans to publish his own work in the near future.

Janice Cohen was born into the world of comics as a Sal Brodsky brat and was reading *Spider-Man* and the *Hulk* even before "Dick & Jane." Naturally, she pursued a career coloring comics. Janice has worked for all the major comic companies for almost fifteen years. A lover of all the arts, she is actively purusing an acting career and has sold lyrics to video documentaries and a feature film. She also grooms dogs on the side.

Stanley Wiater is a media critic, radio commentator, and cineteratologist whose work has appeared in such publications as *Twilight zone, Fangoria,* and *Prevue.* He hopes he can still afford to have Peter Laird continue to design his Christmas cards.

The Feduniewicz Profile:
Name: Ken Feduniewicz
Born: on Deni Loubert's birthday
Schools Attended: Pratt Institute and Joe Kubert School
Last Major Accomplishment: collustration of TMNT
Last Book Read: *Italian Western: The Opera of Violence*
Favorite Heroes: The Holy Trinity: Clint Eastwood, Frank Frazetta, and Elvis Presley
Favorite Film: *Citizen Kane*
Favorite Quote: "Even God must answer to justice."
Major Goal in Life: to have maximum impact with minimal effort
Favorite Drink: it's not Dewar's